Disney's

THE

LION KING

Adapted by Margo Hover

Cover illustration by Niall Harding

Interior illustrations by Judy Barnes and Robbin Cuddy

A Random House PICTUREBACK® Book

Random House 🏠 New York

Copyright © 1994, 2003 Disney Enterprises, Inc. All rights reserved under International and Pan-American Copyright Conventions.
Published in the United States by Random House Children's Books, a division of Random House, Inc., New York,
and simultaneously in Canada by Random House of Canada Limited, Toronto, in conjunction with Disney Enterprises, Inc.
Originally published in slightly different form by Golden Books in 1994. PICTUREBACK, RANDOM HOUSE,
and the Random House colophon are registered trademarks of Random House, Inc.
Library of Congress Control Number: 2002115000
ISBN: 0-7364-2079-7
www.randomhouse.com/kids/disney

Printed in the United States of America   10 9 8 7 6 5 4 3 2 1   First Random House Edition 2003

It was a day of rejoicing on the African plain. All the animals had gathered to witness the presentation of the first cub born to Mufasa, the Lion King, and his queen, Sarabi.

A wise old baboon named Rafiki led the ceremony. Rafiki stood on Pride Rock and held the cub, named Simba, high for all to see.

The animals below were filled with joy. The little creature held so high was the Pride Lands' future king.

Afterward Mufasa went to look for his younger brother, Scar. He found Scar teasing Zazu, the hornbill who was the king's chief minister of affairs.

"Scar, stop it!" ordered Mufasa. Then he asked his brother why he hadn't been at the presentation.

Scar replied angrily that if Simba had not been born, he, Scar, would have been next in line to be king.

In time, Simba grew strong. He stood on Pride Rock to
see the kingdom that would one day be his. "What about
that shadowy place?" asked the cub.

"It's beyond our borders," said Mufasa. "Never go there."
Then he told his son how important it was to be a good
king, one who understood that every creature had a place in
the Circle of Life.

Later that day, before Zazu could prevent it, Simba talked his best friend, Nala, into going on an adventure. They planned to visit that very place where Simba's father had said he must never go.

"Uncle Scar told me about an Elephant Graveyard there!" said Simba excitedly as he and Nala raced along side by side.

When Simba and Nala reached the graveyard, three hyenas appeared. They had been sent by Scar to hunt down Simba.

"There he is," said Shenzi, the leader. "A king fit for a meal."

The cubs ran, only to find themselves trapped in an elephant carcass. Suddenly the Lion King himself appeared. He let out a huge roar, and the hyenas fled.

The angry king sent Nala home with Zazu. As night fell,
he and Simba had a talk.

Simba apologized for disobeying his father. "I was just
trying to be brave," he said.

"Being brave doesn't mean going to look for trouble," said
his father. Then Mufasa explained that the great kings of the
past looked down from the starry sky, ready to guide Simba
whenever he needed help.

Later Scar met with the hyenas. He was furious that they had let the cubs get away. Then he told the hyenas there were going to be some changes. "Mufasa and his son will both die," he said. "Then I will be king, and you will control the Pride Lands!"

The next day Scar lured Simba into a deep gorge, then secretly signaled to the hyenas to start a stampede of wildebeests. Mufasa dragged Simba to safety, but the king was pulled down by the stampede.

As Mufasa struggled to escape, he called out, "Scar, help me."

"Long live the king," answered Scar, pushing his brother to his death below.

When Simba found out his father was dead, he thought it was all his fault. Scar told him there was only one thing to do: "Run, Simba. Run away."

Scar then ordered the hyenas to kill Simba, but the cub escaped through a patch of prickly thorns.

"If you ever come back, we'll kill you!" the hyenas screamed as the terrified cub fled into the jungle.

Scar climbed Pride Rock and announced that both Mufasa and his son were gone forever. He was now king. And the hyenas were welcomed into the Pride Lands.

Simba ran and ran until he was too tired to move.

Fortunately, he was soon rescued by a meerkat named Timon and a warthog named Pumbaa. "He's just a cub," Pumbaa said. "Can we keep him?"

"Are you nuts?" Timon squealed. "Lions eat guys like us!"

In the end, Timon took pity on Simba, and he and Pumbaa dragged the cub into the shade of the jungle.

Simba was soon feeling better, but he could not forget his
last terrible day in the Pride Lands. Timon and Pumbaa tried
to teach him about *hakuna matata*, life without worry.

"No past, no future, no problems, live for today!"
Timon urged.

Simba happily stayed in the jungle with his new friends.

One day Simba went to Pumbaa's rescue when the warthog was attacked by a lioness. As Simba fought off the lioness, he suddenly realized she was Nala, his childhood friend.

"Everyone thinks you're dead," said Nala when she recognized Simba. "I've really missed you."

"I've missed you, too," said Simba.

Later, Nala told Simba about life in the Pride Lands with Scar as king. "There is no food or water," she explained. "If you don't do something, everyone will starve!"

"I can't go back," Simba said. "There's nothing I can do about it. So why worry?"

"Because it's your responsibility!"
Nala told him.

But Simba still believed he had caused
his father's death. He could never show
his face in the Pride Lands again.

That night Simba heard his father's voice. As Simba gazed
up at the star-filled sky, the Lion King said, "You are my son
and the one true king. Now you must take your place in the
Circle of Life."

The vision in the stars began to fade. "Don't leave me!" Simba cried. "Father . . ."

But Mufasa's image was gone, and Simba knew that his father was right. Simba was ready to return to his kingdom.

Before dawn the next day, Nala awakened Timon and
Pumbaa and told them she could not find Simba.

Then they heard a strange voice from a nearby tree. "You
won't find him here," said Rafiki. "The king has returned!"

Nala realized that Simba had gone back to challenge Scar.
Her heart told her to follow Simba home to the Pride Lands.

It was dusk when Simba saw Pride Rock once again. The land around it was parched and dusty.

At the very moment when Simba approached, Scar was in a rage. Many animal herds had long since left the land, and there was nothing left for the lionesses to hunt. In his terrible anger, Scar struck Sarabi, Simba's mother.

Simba confronted Scar. "Either step down or fight!" he commanded.

Scar backed the true Lion King toward the edge of the rock. Simba slipped, but he held on with his front claws. Scar said, "This was just the way your father looked before he died—that is, before I killed him."

"Murderer!" Simba screamed, leaping at Scar.

Simba chased Scar until he begged for mercy. Just as Simba was ready to let him go, Scar lunged at him once more. But Simba was stronger, and his uncle fell to the hard ground below. Scar's terrible reign was over.

As his mother and friends watched, Simba claimed his kingdom.

Peace returned to the Pride Lands, and the Circle of Life continued when a cub was born to Queen Nala and King Simba.

On the day of the presentation at Pride Rock, Rafiki lifted the cub high for all to see, just as he had lifted Simba many years before.